GIVING UP THE GHOST

Teatro in Two Acts

by Cherríe Moraga

West End Press

Giving Up the Ghost was performed in an earlier version as a staged
reading at the Foot of the Mountain Theatre of Minneapolis in June
1984. As the work (at publication) has not been produced, stage
directions have been kept to a minimum. Those interested in pro-
ducing *Giving Up the Ghost* should write the author for permission
through the publisher.

Photo: Annette Pelaez
Artistic conception: Osa Hidalgo de la Riva
Cover design: Sherri Holtke

First edition – August, 1986
ISBN 0-931122-43-0

This project is partially supported by a grant from
the National Endowment for the Arts, a federal agency.

West End Press
P.O. Box 291477
Los Angeles, California 90029

Giving Up the Ghost

If I had wings like an angel
over these prison walls
I would fly

(song my mother would sing me)

THE CHARACTERS

MARISA   Chicana in her late 20s
CORKY   MARISA's younger self, at 11 and 17 years old
AMALIA   Chicana in her late 40s, born in México
THE PEOPLE   Those viewing THE PERFORMANCE

CORKY is "una chaparrita" who acts tough, but has a wide open sincerity in her face which betrays the toughness.   She dresses in the "cholo style" of her period (the '60s): khakis with razor-sharp creases; pressed white undershirt; hair short and slicked back.

MARISA, over 10 years later, wears her toughness less self-consciously, a little closer to the bone.   The sincerity is more guarded.   She appears in levis, tennis shoes, and a dark shirt. Her hair is short.

AMALIA is "soft" in just the ways that MARISA is "hard."   Her clothes give the impression of being draped, as opposed to worn. Shawl-over-blouse-over-skirt — all of Mexican Indian design.   Her hair is long and worn down or loosely braided.   There is nothing frivolous about this woman.

The STAGE SET should be black with as few props as possible. Crates, platforms, or simple wooden chairs, for example, should be used to represent "the street," a "bed," "kitchen," etc.   Lighting should be the main feature in providing setting. Throughout the long monologues (unless otherwise stated), the lighting should give the impression that the ACTORS are within hearing range of one another; that THEY in fact know what the other is saying (thinking), even when there is no obvious response from the "listener."

The ACTION (story) takes place (not chronologically) over a period of months.
The place: East Los Angeles
The year: 1980

ACT ONE
"LA PACHUCA"

Dedicación

Don't know where this woman and I
will find each other again,
but I am grateful to her   to something
that feels like a blessing

that I am, in fact,
not *trapped*

which brings me to the question of prisons
politics
sex.

Music.

Voice from the dark.

MARISA
I'm only telling you this to stay my hand.

Lights slowly come up on MARISA downstage center, facing THE PEOPLE. CORKY sits back-to-back with MARISA. SHE is not yet visible.

But why, cheezus, why me?
Why'd I hafta get into a situation
where all my ghosts come to visit?

I always see that man — thick-skinned, dark, muscular.
He is a boulder between us.
I cannot lift him and her, too, carrying him.

He is a ghost, always haunting her . . .
lingering.

MARISA slowly exits.

'60s Chicano-style rock 'n' roll can be heard as CORKY turns to face THE PEOPLE. SHE "moves with it" until it slowly fades out.

CORKY (1963)
*the smarter I get the older I get the meaner I get
tough   a tough cookie my mom calls me
sometimes I even pack a blade   no one knows
I never use it or nut'ing but can feel it there
there in my pants pocket   run the pad of my thumb over it
to remind me I carry some'ting   am sharp   secretly
always envy those batos who get all cut up at the weddings
getting their rented tuxes all bloody
that red 'n' clean color against the white
starched collars   I love that shit!*

*the best part is the chicks
all climbing into the ball of the fight
Chuey déjalo!   leave him go, Güero!
tú sabes   you know how the chicks get
all excited 'n' upset 'n' stuff
they always pulling on the carnales 'n' getting
nowhere 'cept messed up themselves 'n' everybody
looks so like they digging the whole t'ing   tú sabes
their dresses ripped here 'n' there . . . like a movie*

it's all like a movie

4

when I was a little kid I useta love the movies
every saturday you could find me there
my eyeballs glued to the screen
then during the week my friend Tudy and me
we'd make up our own movies
one of our favorites was this cowboy one
where we'd be out in the desert
'n' we'd capture these chicks 'n' hold 'em up
for ransom   we'd string 'em up 'n'
make 'em take their clothes off
jus' pretend a'course but it useta make me feel
real tough
strip   we'd say to the wall
all cool-like

funny now when I think about how little I was
at the time   and a girl
but in my mind   I was big 'n' tough 'n' a dude
in my mind   I had all their freedom
the freedom to really see a girl
kinda   the way   you see
an   animal   you know?

like imagining
they got a difernt set
of blood vessels
or somet'ing   like   so
when you mess with 'em

5

it don' affect 'em
the way   it do   you
like   like they got a difernt
gland system   or somet'ing   that
that   makes their pain cells
more dense

hell I dunno

but you see
I never could
quite
pull it off

always knew I was a girl
deep down inside
no matter how
I tried to pull the other
off

I knew

always knew

I was an animal that kicked back

cuz it hurt

Black out.

6

MARISA is sitting on top of her "bed" stage left, rubbing her calves.

MARISA
I'm not tryin' to make no big deal outta this.
In fact, I been avoiding making any deal at all.
But when I go to sleep my legs stiffen up on me
like they got rocks in them.
I mean it. No kinda stretching can release the rock
ball of hardness I got locked between my knees 'n' ankles.

I stretch them.
Dig my bone fingers into the meat of the calf to work it out.
Me duele pero there's no relaxing them.
I'm forced outta bed with the pain.
Marta finds me cruisin' the house like a damn
                        sleep-walking zombie.
"You can't sleep, Marisa?" she tries.
"No, I can't," I cry
cuz I'm fighting in my legs what I know.
I'm standing firm on the ground even when I'm layin'
                        sideways up in bed
cuz I'm sure to fly away in this anger,
no root to it at all.
Bottomless.
Bottomless.

What *is* betrayal?
Let me tell you about it, it is not clean, nothing neat.
It's about a battle I will never win and never stop fighting.

The dick beats me every time.

I know I'm not supposed to be sayin' this
cuz it's like confession,
it's like still cryin' your sins to a priest you long ago
stopped believing was god or god's sit-in.
And you? Pues, you aint no soldier of christ,
but still confessing what long ago you hoped
would be forgiven in you, that prison
that passion
to beat them
at their own game.

AMALIA *(entering stage right)*
I worry about La Pachuca.
That's my nickname for her.
I have trouble calling her by her Christian name, Marisa.
It's a beautiful name, really, but she defies it at every turn.
In fact, I change her name at regular intervals
just to stay abreast with her.
La quiero mucho.
She doesn't always know it,
pero hay parte de ella misma que lo sabe perfectamente.

I worry about La Pachuca.
I worry what will happen to the beautiful corn
                                        she is growing
if it continues to rain so hard and much.

8

CORKY *(downstage center, sitting)*
one time Tudy and me did it for real
strip   I mean
we been playing these movie capture games 'n' all
'n' getting ourselves all worked-up
I mean we could play these games for days!

anyway there was this minister 'n' his family down the street
they was presbyterians or methodists or somet'ing
you know one of those gringo religions
and they had a bunch a kids
the oldest was named Lisa or somet'ing lightweight like that
and the littlest was about three or so named Chrissy
I mean you couldn't really complain about Chrissy
cuz she wasn't old enough yet to be a pain in the cola
but you knew that was coming

Lisa'd be hassling me and my sister Patsy all the time
tell us how we wernt really christians cuz cath-lics
worshipped the virgin mary or somet'ing
I dint let this worry me too much though cuz
we was being tole at school how being cath-lic was
the one true numero uno church 'n' all
so I just let myself be real cool with her
'n' the rest of her little pagan baby brothers 'n' sisters
that's all they was to me as far as I was concerned

they dint even have no mass   jus' some paddy preaching
up on their altar with a dark suit on
very weird
not a damn candle for miles
dint seem to me that there was any god
                              happening in that place at all

9

so back to Tudy and me
one day Tudy comes up with this idea how we should strip for real
well   I wasn't that hot on the idea but still go along with him
hopping from backyard to backyard looking for prey
then we run into Chrissy
so Tudy 'n' me eye each other 'n' figure
she's the perfect victim
for our sick little fantasies

the trouble is   I'm still not completely sold on the idea
but Tudy was always too stupid to pull anything off by himself
so I end up working out the whole damn thing
            the boy lacked imagination if you know what I mean

Chrissy is hanging out in her backyard
they have this kinda shed there
with a buncha junk in it that nobody used for nut'ing
so I say to her real simple-minded like   all syrupy-mouthed
come heeeeere Chrissy   we got somet'ing to shooooow you
well a'course the kid comes cuz I was a big kid 'n' all
so we take her into the shed

I have her hand 'n' Tudy tells her
(as if suddenly remembering)
            no   I told her this
I tell her we think she's got somet'ing wrong with her
"down there"
I think   I think I said she had a coco or somet'ing
'n' Tudy 'n' me had to check it out
so I pull her little shorts down
'n' then her chonas
'n' then jus' as we catch a glimple of her little
            fuchi fachi . . .

it was so tender-looking
all pink 'n' real sweet
like a bun
'n' then Tudy like a pendejo
goes 'n' sticks his dirty finger on it
like it was burning hot
'n' jus' at that moment . . .

I see this little Chrissy-kid look up at me
> *like*
> *like I was her mom or somet'ing*
> *like   tú sabes*
she has this little kid's frown on her face
> *like*
> *like she knew*

somet'ing was wrong with what we was up to
'n' was looking at me to reassure her
that everything was cool
'n' regular 'n' all

what a pendeja I felt like

so I swipe Tudy's stupid hand away 'n' say
"let's get outta here!"
'n' pull up her shorts 'n' whisper to her
"no no you're fine   really
there's nothing wrong with you
but don' tell nobody we looked
it's a secret
we don' want nobody to worry
about you"
> *what else was I supposed to say?*

11

(to herself)   tonta
'n' Tudy 'n' me make a beeline into the alley
'n' outta there

(long pause, coming toward THE PEOPLE)
the weird thing was
that after that I was like a maniac all summer
snotty Lisa kept harassing me about the virgin mary
'n' all 'n' jus' in general being a pain in the coolie

things began to break down when me 'n' Patsy stopped
going to their church meetings on wednesday nights
we'd only go cuz they had cookies 'n' treats
after all the bible stuff
'n' sometimes had arts 'n' crafts where you got to paint
little clay statues of blonde Jesus in a robe
'n' the little children coming to him

anyway the reason we stopped going was cuz
one time during these "prayer meetings" they called 'em
where everybody'd stand in a circle
squeezing hands and each kid'd say a little prayer
you know like for the starving people in china
      Patsy and me always passed
      jus' shaked our heads no when we got squeezed
      cuz it was against our religion 'n' all to pray with them
well one time this Lisa punk has the nerve to pray
that Patsy 'n' me would
(mimicking) "come to the light
of the one true christian faith"
shi-it   can you get to that?
'course we never went again

I 'member coming home 'n' telling my mom
'n' she says "it's better mi'jitas
I think if you don' go no more"

'n' it was so nice to hear her voice
so warm like she loved us a lot

'n' that night
being cath-lic felt like my mom

real warm 'n' dark 'n' kind

MARISA *(long pause)*
I hate men.
Ya, I said it.
Like my roommate, Marta, she said it too yesterday
ironing her blouse for work
the one I had just fixed a hole in,
"You know Marisa, men are truly not worth
getting your hands dirty."
This time she hates them because she jerked
one of our co-workers off, just this nobody
guy with muscles on the night-shift,
literally, with her free hand on her free time
and now he thinks he's got something over on her
and it was the easiest thing jerking him around.
"Men are easy," she says, "always easier than women."
No challenge to them at all.

I never wanted to be a man
I only wanted a woman to want me that bad.
And they have, you know, plenty of them,
but there's always that one you can't pin down
who's undecided.

My mother was a heterosexual
I couldn't save her.
My failures follow thereafter.

AMALIA   *(seated in her "kitchen" stage right)*
I am a failure.
I see them.
Their security.   Their houses.   Their dogs.
Their children are happy.   They are not *un*-happy.
Sure they have their struggles, their problemas, but . . .

It's a life.
I always say this.
"It's a life."

MARISA
Marta bought her mother a house.
After the family talked bad about her
for leaving Chihuahua with a gavacha
she returned cash in hand and bought her mother a casita
kinda on the outskirts of town
ten grand was all it took, that's nothing here
but it did save her mother from the poverty
her dead father left behind.
Her brother didn't do that.
La admiro.
For the first time wished my father dead

14

so I could do my mother that kind
of rescue routine.

She, the one I could never pin down,
said to me very sweetly-like . . .

AMALIA
I feel like the little bird that was nesting
in the palm of my hand has flown away.

MARISA
That's me, the pajarita with legs like steel planks in my bed.
(rubbing)   Is it my anger that keeps me bolted to this planet?

The women I have loved the most
have always loved the man more than me,
even in their hatred of them.
I'm queer I am.   Sí soy jota
because I have never ever been crazy about a man.

My friend Sally, the hooker,
she still calls herself that even though she aint doin it
no more, she told me the day she decided
to stop tricking was when once, by accident
a john made her come.
That was strickly forbidden, she explained to me,
how her co-workers who were also dykes had this pact.
She'd forgotten to resist.
To keep business, business.
She had let herself go.
It was very *un*-professional
and dangerous.

15

No, I've never been in love with a man.
I never understood women who were,
although I've certainly been around
to pick up the pieces.

(CORKY approaches MARISA.   THEY count off in unison)
My sister was in love with my brother.
My mother loved her father.
My first woman, the man who put her away.

CORKY
The crazy house.   Camarillo, Califas.   1968.

MARISA
When I come to get Norma, she has eyes
like saucers   spinning black and glass
I can see through them
my face   my name
she says,
     "I am buddha."

How'd you get those black eyes
is all I wanna know.

     "¿Quién te pegó?" I ask.
     "I am buddha."

Black out.

CORKY *(downstage center)*
since that prayer meeting night
Lisa had been on the warpath
her nose getting higher 'n' higher in the air
one day Patsy 'n' her are playing dolls
up on the second-story porch of Mrs. Rodriguez' house
it was nice up there cuz Mrs. R would let you
move the tables 'n' chairs 'n' stuff around
so you could really make it like a house if you wanted to
my sister had jus' gotten this nice doll for her birthday
it had this great curly hair
Lisa had only this kinda stupid doll with plastic
painted-on hair 'n' only one leg
she'd always hafta wear long dresses on it
to disguise the missing leg but we all knew it was gone
anyway one day this brat Lisa throws my sister's new doll
into this mud puddle right down from Mrs. R's porch
Patsy comes back into our yard crying like crazy
her doll's all muddy and the hair has turned bone straight
I mean like an arrow!
I wanted to kill that punk Lisa!
so me 'n' Patsy go over to Lisa's house where we find the little creep
all pleased with herself I mean not even feeling bad

suddenly I see her bike which is really her tricycle
but it's huge . . . I mean hu-u-uge!
to this day I never seen a trike that big
don't even think they make 'em that big no more
no more babies big enough

17

it useta irritate me to no end that she wasn't even trying
to learn to ride a two-wheeler
so all of a sudden that bike and Lisa's wimpiness
comes together in my mind and I got that t'ing and threw
the sucker into the middle of the street
I dint even wreck it none

but it was the principle of the t'ing.

the drag was a'course she goes 'n' tells her mom on me
'n' this lady who by my mind don' even seem like a mom
she dint wear no makeup 'n' was real skinny 'n' tall
'n' wore her hair all long 'n' tied up in some kind of dumb bun
anyway she has the nerve to call my mom 'n' tell her what I done
so a'course my mom calls me on the carpet wants to know the story
'n' I tell her 'bout the doll 'n' Pasty 'n' the principle of the t'ing
'n' Patsy's telling the same story 'n' I can see in my mom's eye
she don' really believe I did nothing so bad
but she tells me how she wants to keep peace in the neighborhood
cuz we was already getting hassles from some of the paddy neighbors
about how my mom hollered too much at us kids . . . her own kids!
I mean if you can't yell at your own kids who can you yell at?
but she don' let on that this is the reason but I could tell
by the way my mom wasn't looking me in the face when she tells me
I hafta go over to the minister's house 'n' apologize
she jus' kinda turns back to the stove 'n' keeps on with
what she was doing telling me "ándale mi'ja dinner's almost ready."

so a'course I go . . . I remember . . . I go by myself
with no one to watch me to see if I really do it

but my mom knows I will cuz she tole me to
'n' I ring the doorbell 'n' Mrs. Minister answers
'n' as I begin to talk I guess the little wimp hears my voice
'n' runs up behind her mother's skirt 'n' peeks out at me
from behind it with the ugliest most snottiest shit-eating grin
I'd ever seen in a person.

all the while I say I'm sorry
'n' as the door shuts in front of my face
I vow I'll never make a mistake like that again . . .

I'll never show anybody how mad I can get.

Black out.   Corky exits.

MARISA
I have a very long memory.
I try to warn people how when I get hurt,
I don't forget it
never really let it go.
I use it against them.

I blame women for everything,
for my mistakes
missed opportunities
for my grief.

I usually leave just before I wanna lay a woman flat.
When I feel that rise up in me,
that vengeance
that getting-backness,
I run muddy river.
I book.
Hop a train.
Split.
Desert.

AMALIA
Desert. Desierto.
Maybe in the desert, it could have turned out
differently between La Pachuca and me.
I *had* intended to take her there,
to México.

She would never have gone alone,
sin gente allí.

For some reason, I could always picture
her in the desert
amid the mesquite y nopal.
Always when I closed my eyes to search for her,
it was in the desert where I found her,

but once with eyes open
I actually did see her there,
en el desierto
there in the body of a little girl.

I was on a bus headed south
traveling through what turned
from U.S. desert to México,
but all was México
        my bones remembered.
(sadly)
        It was to be my last trip.
        I felt this, for some reason, unspeakably.

But there was my niña,
her head stuck all the way out of the bus window,
drinking in the hot desert air.
Her hair
flapping in the wind of it
black and dancing.

She is singing and I am putting
La Pachuca's words in her mouth

(AMALIA comes up behind MARISA, wraps her arms around her
neck, sings)
        "Desierto de la Sonora
        Tierra de mi memoria"

Sí
Sí ésas son tu raíces mi chula.
(whispering)
Cántales.   Cántales.
Same chata face.   Yaqui.

(almost like a chant)
La luz del atardecer.
Las sierras son azules y lloran en esta luz.
Hay un silencio que habla de cosas ancianas.
Secretos enterrados.
Nada se mueve,
como yo,
pero todo suspira
"Mi chata.
Mi amor."

MARISA
(unmoved)
I've just never believed
a woman capable of loving a man
was capable of loving a woman
me.

Some part of me remains amazed
that I'm not the only lesbian in the world
and that over the years I can always manage
to find someone
to love me.

But I am never satisfied
because there are always those women left,
unloved.

I don't get it.
I just feel there is a cruel unfairness
in this world, this division
between love
and labor.

AMALIA drops her hands from MARISA's shoulders, coming toward THE PEOPLE. Long pause.

AMALIA
I've only gone crazy over one man in my life.
He was nothing special.
Pescador. Indio.
Worked the same waters his whole life.
Once we took a drive out of the small town he lived in,
and he was like a baby, terrified.

Era increíble.
I'm driving through the mountains
and he's squirming in his seat,
"Amalia, ¿pa' dónde vamos? Are you sure you know
where we're going?" he kept asking.
I was so amused to see this big macho break
out into a cold sweat
just from going no more than twenty some miles
from his home town.

Pero, ¡ Ay Dios! How I loved that man!
I still ask myself what I saw in him, really.
(pause) He was one of the cleanest people I had ever met.
Took two, three baths a day.
You have to, you know.
That part of la costa is like steam baths some seasons.
I remember how he'd even put powder in his shorts
and under his huevos to keep dry.
He was *that* clean.
I always loved knowing that when I touched him,
I would find him like a saint.

23

Pure, somehow.
That no matter where he had been or who he had been with,
he would have washed himself for me.
He always smelled . . . como flor.

Me volví loca over this man, literally.
When I returned home after so many years,
                                    I had never dreamed

of falling in love,
too many damn men under the bridge.

I can see them all floating down the river
like so many sacks of potatoes.
To me, each one . . .
making love they call it
was like having sex with children.
They rub your chi-chis a little,
put their finger in you to get you a little wet,
then they stick it in you.
Nada más.
It's all over in a few minutes.
Un río de cuerpos muertos.

MARISA *(to AMALIA)*
Sometimes I only see the other river on your face.
I see it running behind your eyes.
Remember the time we woke up together
and your eye was a bowl of blood.
I thought the river had broken open inside you.

AMALIA
I was crazy about Alejandro. Muy loca.
Now I wonder how it was he put up with me.
But what I loved was not so much him,
I loved his children.
I loved the part of México that was my home with him,

the way he had made México my home again.

Los pájaros eran Alejandro.
El Alejandro was the birds, the insects that
that first summer never bit me.

I, on the other hand, was not clean,
forgot sometimes to wash.
Not when I was around others,
pero con mi misma, I became like the animals
uncombed, el olor del suelo.

MARISA
I remember the story she told me about the village children,
how they had put a muñeca under the door of her casita
how she had found it there.
It was the first time she had appeared
mad to herself.

So, we take each other in doses.
I learn to swallow my desire,
work my fear slowly through
the strands of her hair.

(to AMALIA)
When I saw the seaweed in long thick
strands swaying back and forth
a deep blue brown against green ocean
and foaming lip of white,

I saw *you* there
underwater

the seaweed era tu pelo
heavy with movement
ola y piedra
and I nearly lost my balance
on the salt cliff
that held me

But when the fear gripped me, that sharp stab
of panic you get in the pit of your belly,
I suddenly saw you so different.
The hair pulled from your face,
the head dangling, suspended.

Bruja, pensé.
Vieja.
Mala suerte.
I felt so ashamed to see you like that,
if only in my mind.
Can you forgive me?

AMALIA
Am I your confessor?
Your priest?

MARISA
No, it's only that I felt I had betrayed you
in my thoughts.

AMALIA
Your thoughts are yours.
They speak of you, not me
mi corazón.

MARISA
But then was the beautiful woman
in the mirror of the water
you or me?

Who do I make love to?
Who do I see in the ocean of our bed?

Long pause.

AMALIA   *(sitting, to THE PEOPLE)*
When I learned of Alejandro's death,
I died too, weeks later.
I just started bleeding and the blood wouldn't stop,
not until his ghost had passed through me
or was born in me
I don't know which.

(pause)   Except since then,
I feel him living in me
every time I touch la Marisa
I don't know he's been there
until I put my teeth to her flesh.

27

That morning I awoke to find the sheets red with blood.
It had come out in torrents and then
in thick clots that looked close to a fetus.
But I had not been pregnant,
my tubes tied for years now.
And lying there among the cool dampness of my own blood,
I felt my womanhood leave me.
Does this make sense?
And it was Alejandro being born in me.
I can't say exactly why or how I knew this,
except again for the smell, the unmistakable
smell of the sex of the man
as if we had just made love
el olor estaba en el aire
alrededor de la cama
and coming from my lips was *his* voice
"¡Ay mi Marisa! ¡Te deseo! ¡Te deseo!"

MARISA
If I had been a man,
things would of been a lot simpler between us,
except for one thing . . .
she never would of wanted me.
I mean she would of seen me more and all,
fit me more conveniently into her life

but she never would of, tú sabes . . .
wanted me.

It's odd being queer.
It's not that you don't want a man,
you just don't want a man in a man.
You want a man in a woman.
The woman-part goes without saying.
That's what you always learn to want first.
Maybe the first time you see
your Dad touch your Mom
in that way . . .

CORKY *(entering)*
Eeeho! I remember the first time I got hip to that!
my mom standing at the stove making chile colorado or somet'ing
she asking my dad did he want another tortilla
" ¿quieres otro viejo?" she asks
kinda like she's sorta hassled 'n' being poquita fría
tú sabes but she's really digging my dad to no end
'n' he knows it and nods 'n' jus' as she comes over to him
kinda flipping the tort onto the plate he grabs her
between her step 'n' slides his hand up the inside of her thigh
cheeezus! I coulda died!
I musta been only 'bout nine or so but I got that tingling
tú sabes that now I know what it means . . .

CORKY throws chin out to MARISA bato-style. MARISA, amused, returns it. CORKY exits.

MARISA *(watching AMALIA)*
Cuando Amalia me dijo . . .

AMALIA *(to MARISA)*
Quítate tus pantalones.

MARISA *(to THE PEOPLE)*
I obey and slide off my pants.
Me siento como un joven lleno de deseo.

The worn denim and metal buttons
are cotton and cool ice on my skin.
I move on top of her, she wants this
and she is full of slips and lace and stockings
and yet it is *she* who's taking *me*.

> *(watching AMALIA)*
> Hay un hombre en esa mujer
> lo he sentido
> la miro, haciendo cafe para nosotras
> frente a hornilla
> pienso . . .
> *¿como puedo ver un hombre en una persona*
> *tan hembra?*
>
> El pelo
> sus movimientos

de una quietud imposible describir
la voz que me acaricia con cada palabra
tan suave, tan rica.

Pienso en mi mamá.
Había un hombre en mi mamá también.

(pause, to THE PEOPLE)
After the last tequila and the first long kiss
into the side of her grey face, she warned . . .

AMALIA
Don't do that.   I just can't afford to feel it now.

MARISA
. . . and I wanted to plunge my hands into every opening
her body knew.

But it's not the desire for my touch which drives her,
but the need to touch me.
"Let's go home," I say.

(coming toward AMALIA)
I held the moment.
Strained, that if I looked long and hard enough
at the woman's hand full inside me
if beneath the moon blasting through the window
I could picture and hold pictured in my mind

(MARISA takes AMALIA's hand)
how that hand buried in the wool of my hair
her working it, herself, into me
how everything was changing at that moment
in both of us.

MARISA and AMALIA   *(to each other)*
How everything was changing
in both of us.

Black out.

End of Act One.

ACT TWO
"LA SALVADORA"

Dedicación 2

I have this rock in my hand
it is my memory
no one can take it away from me

the weight is dense, solid
in my palm   it cannot fly away

and I still remember
that
woman
    not my savior
    but an angel
    with wings
    that did once lift me
    to another
    self.

Voices from the dark, like a memory.

AMALIA
You have the rest of your life to forgive me.

MARISA
Forgive you for what?

AMALIA
My ways.

Music.
It is 1969.
CORKY enters to downstage center, straddling a crate. Something in her appearance or style should give the impression that she is now six years older. She is slightly more subdued.

The music gradually subsides. After a pause, CORKY begins slowly.

Got raped once.
When I was a kid.
Taken me a long time to say that was exactly what happened,
but that was exactly what happened.
Makes you more aware than ever that you are one hunerd percent
female, just in case you had any doubts
one hunerd percent female whether you act it or like it or not.

Y'see I never ever really let myself think about it
the possibility of rape   even after it happened.
Not like other girls I dint walk down the street
like they was men lurking everywhere every corner to devour you.
Yeah, the street was a war zone but for difernt reasons,
for muggers, Mexicanos sucking their damn lips at you,
gringo stupidity, drunks like old garbage sacks
                              thrown around the street
and the rape of other women and the people I loved.
They wernt safe and I worried each time they left the house,
but never never me.

I guess I never wanted to believe I was raped.
If it could happen to me, I'd rather think it was something else
like "unprovoked" sex or something   hell I dunno.
But if someone took me that bad, I wouldn't really want to think
I was took   you follow me?

But the truth is . . . I was took.

CORKY begins to walk about downstage as she tells "the story."

I was about twelve years old,
can even see my little body back then.
Chaparrita.
We wore these kind of jumpers, tú sabes, the kind
they always have for cath-lic school.
They looked purty shitty on the seventh 'n' eighth grade girls
cuz here we was getting chi-chis 'n' all 'n' still trying
to shove 'em into the tops of these jumpers.
I wasn't too big, tú sabes, pero the big girls looked te-rri-ble!

Anyway in the seventh grade I was trying to mend my ways
so would hang after school 'n' try to be helpful 'n' all to the nuns.
I guess cuz my older cousin Norma got straight A's
'n' was taking me into her bed by then
so I figured . . . that was the way to go.

She'd get really pissed when I fucked up in school,
threatened to "take it away" tú sabes if I dint behave.
Can you get to that? ¡Qué fría! ¿no?

Anyway Norma was the only one I ever tole about the custodian
doing it to me 'n' then she took it away for good.
I'd still like to whip her butt for that
her 'n' her goddamn hubby 'n' kids now   shi-it
puros gavachos   little blonde-haired blue-eyed things.

The oldest is a little joto if you ask me.
Sure, he's barely four years old, but you can already tell
the way he goes around primping all over the place.
Pleases me to no end.
What goes around, comes around.
"Jason," they call him.
No, not "Hasón," pero "Jay-sun."
Puro gringo.

Anyway so I was walking by Sister Mary Dominic's classroom,
"The Hawk" we called her cuz she had a nose 'n' attitude like one
when this man, a mexicano, motions to me to come on inside.
I'm looking for this girl Rosie who said she'd meet me
cuz she has something "very important" to tell me.
So this guy calls me, "Ven p'aca," he says.
He's about in his late thirties, I dint recognize him
but the parish was always hiring mexicanos to work
around the grounds 'n' stuff I guess cuz they dint need
to know English 'n' the priests dint need to pay 'em much.
They'd do it "por Dios" tú sabes.
So he asks me if I speak Spanish.
"Señorita ¿hablas español?" muy humilde y todo
'n' I answer, "Sí, poquito," which I always say to strangers
cuz I dunno how much will be expected of me.

"Ven p'aca," he says otra vez 'n' I do outta respect
for my primo Enrique cuz he looks alot like him, real neatly dressed.
He had work clothes on 'n' all I remember but they wernt dirty
or wrinkled or nuthin like they shoulda been
if he'd been working all day
but he has this screwdriver in his hand
so I figure he must be legit.
But something was funny, and his Spanish . . .

38

I couldn't quite make it out cuz he mumbled alot
which made me feel kinda bad about myself tú sabes
that I was Mexican too but couldn't understand him that good.
So, I mostly jus' catch on by his body movements
what he wants me to do.

He's tryin' to fix this drawer that's loose in the Hawk's desk.
I knew already about the drawer cuz she was always bitching
'n' moaning about it getting stuck cuz the bottom kept falling out.
So, he tells me he needs someone to hold the bottom
of the drawer up so he can screw the sides in
which makes sense to me, but the problem is . . .
I don' see no screws.
Looked to me like the whole damn thing was glued together.
¡Qué tonta soy! ¿no?

But standing to the side, I lean over
and hold the drawer up with my hand, así.
(CORKY demonstrates)
Then he says all frustrated-like, "No, así, así."
It turns out he wants me to stand in front of the drawer
with my hands holding each side up 'n' my legs apart,
así. (she demonstrates)
'n' believe it or not, I do
'n' believe it or not, this hijo de la chingada madre
sits behind me on the floor 'n' reaches his arm up
between my legs that I'm straining to keep closed
even though he keeps saying all business-like
"Abrete más, por favor, las piernas. Abrete poco más, señorita."
Still all polite 'n' like a pendeja . . . I do.
Little by little, he gets my legs open.

39

I feel my face getting hotter 'n' I can kinda feel him
jiggling the drawer pressed up against my front part.
I'm staring straight ahead don' wanna look at what's happening
then worry how someone would see us like this this guy's arm
up between my legs 'n' then it begins to kinda brush
past the inside of my thigh   his arm   I can feel the hair
that first   then the heat of his skin 'n' I keep wishing 'n' dreading
that my stupid friend Rosie with her stupid secret might come by.

The skin
the skin is so soft I hafta admit
young kinda . . . like a girl's like . . . Norma's shoulder.
I try to think about Norma 'n' her shoulders
to kinda pass the time hoping to hurry things along
while he keeps saying, "casi término, casi término"
'n' I keep saying back,
"señor me tengo que ir mi mamá me espera"
still all polite como mensa
until finally I feel the screwdriver by my leg like ice
then suddenly the tip of it   it feels like to me
is against the cotton of my chonas.

"Don't move," he tells me.   In English.   His accent gone.
'n' I don.'

(SHE moves right down to the center of THE PEOPLE).
From then on all I see in my mind's eye . . .
          were my eyes shut?
is this screwdriver he's got in his sweaty palm
yellow   glass   handle
shiny   metal
the kind my father useta use to fix things around the house

40

remembered how I'd help him
how he'd take me on his jobs with him
'n' I kept getting him confused in my mind this man 'n' his arm
with my father   kept imagining him my father returned
come back
the arm was so soft   but this other thing . . .
hielo   hielo   ice
I wanted to cry "papá papá" 'n' then I started crying for real
cuz I knew I musta done something real wrong to get myself
in this mess.

I figure he's gonna shove the damn thing up me
he's trying to get my chonas down 'n' I jus' keep saying
"por favor señor no please don' "
but I can hear my voice through my own ears
not from the inside out but the other way around
'n' I know I'm not fighting this one I know
I don' even sound convinced.

"¿Dónde 'stás papá?" I keep running through my mind
"¿dónde 'stás?"
'n' finally I imagine the man answering
"aquí estoy.   soy tu papá."
'n' this gives me permission to go 'head
to not hafta fight.

By the time he gets my chonas down to my knees
I suddenly feel like I'm walking on air
like I been exposed to the air   like I have no kneecaps
my thing kinda not attached to no body
flapping in the wind like a bird
a wounded bird.

41

I'm relieved when I hear the metal drop to the floor
only worry   who will see me doing this?
get-this-over-with-get-this-over-with
'n' he does gracias a dios bringing his hand up
bringing me down to earth
linoleum floor   cold
the smell of wax polish.

Y ya 'stoy lista for what long ago waited for me
there was no surprise
"open your legs" me dijo otra vez
'n' I do cuz I'm not useta fighting
what feels
like resignation

what feels
like the most natural thing in the world
to give in

'n' I open my legs wide wide open
for the angry animal that springs outta the opening
in his pants 'n' all I wanna do is have it over
so I can go back to being myself 'n' a kid again.

Then he hit me with it
into what was supposed to be a hole
that I remembered had to be cuz Norma had found it
once wet 'n' forbidden 'n' showed me too
how wide 'n' deep like a cueva
hers got when she wanted it to
only with me she said   (pause)
"Only with you, Corky."

But with this one
there was no hole
he had to make it
'n' I saw myself down there like a face
with no opening
a face with no features
no eyes no nose no mouth
only little lines where they shoulda been
so I dint cry

I never cried as he shoved the thing
into what was supposed to be a mouth
with no teeth
with no hate
with no voice
only a hole.   A Hole!
(gritando)
HE MADE ME A HOLE!

Black out.

MARISA   (upstage, after a pause)
I don't regret it.
I don't regret nuthin.
He only convinced me of my own name.
From an early age you learn to live with it,
being a woman . . .
I only got a head start over some.

And then, years later
after I got to be with some other men,
I admired how their things had no opening,

43

only a tiny tiny pinhole dot to pee from, to come from.
I thought . . . how lucky they were
that they could release all that stuff,
all that pent-up shit from the day
through a hole
that nobody . . . could get into.

MARISA turns away from THE PEOPLE and slowly exits.

Silence.

AMALIA   *(entering "the street" downstage)*
En la Zona Rosa, the sky remains pink in light
in night life.
My novio from many years ago is beside me.
I link my arm into his.
(begins to walk as if with a "partner")
We have found each other once again
in the country of our birth.
Somos mexicanos still returning.
I am pleased that we have run into each other
no need to explain
what kind of almas perdidas somos.
At least, tonight
no need to explain.

Carlos is cardboard,
not because he has no feeling,
but I attribute no feeling to him.   His eyes
may bleed in their want
to know, sorrow to see me
suffer so.
I am shocked it is so visible on my skin
pero no puedo sentirlo.
No puedo.

But we walk together arm in arm
with the generosity of old lovers.
He asks nothing of me and I pray
the cobblestones beneath my feet
la memoria de la piedra abajo
will return the life to me
(pause)
but I have already lost this life,
this man.
Ya me abandoné.

So I stop him in the middle of our walk,
grab his two hands in mine,
and ask him to make love to me
the best way he knows how.
He is a beautiful passionate man, really.
I can see this on the screen of his face,
muy mexicano.

He was my first latino lover and it is true
this makes a difference . . . older now,
both of us, gris y maduro
like this ground that weeps
beneath these buildings,
campo frágil
con memoria tan violente que
podría destruir todos de estos edificios.
U.S. Embassy. Banco Serfin. Cocktail lounge.
Curio shop.

"Regresaré." La Tierra nos recuerda.
"Regresaré." Nos promete.

When they "discovered" El Templo Mayor
beneath the walls of this city,
they had not realized that it was she
who discovered them.
Nothing remains buried forever.
Not even memory.
Especially, not even memory.

Pero, Carlos . . .
Carlos takes me back to my hotel room.
I credit him with a power only his race remembers.
In spite of himself, todavía lo tiene.
La Raza recuerda.

He is a good lover, we enter our bed confidently.
He takes me into his arms . . . first with his clothes on
which mexicanos are likely to do. We love
the ritual of the unveiling.

He is already stirring beneath
the flannel of his professor's pants.
He is still a boy after all.
Me encanta for his sake.
Men go from boys to viejos . . . todavía es chavo.

I wonder for a moment . . . *what moves him?*
¿La memoria?
¿La nostalgia para nuestra juventud?
¿La esperanza para alguna mujer mágia
que lo puede salvar de su propia vergüenza?

We take to bed the gavacha wife
the twenty-five-year-old marriage.
What breed of man we produce!
For a moment, he is like my son and I fear
I should have taken better care with him.
Men go from boys to viejos
(sighing) so soon.

I don't stop thinking of the wife.
I offer to her through his hungry rose mouth
my pezones, withered as they are.
I offer them
that someone
might keep watch
continue dreaming
that our mouths and tongues and enflaming nerves
can cleanse us of our feelings,
our shame.

47

Carlos tells me,
"Te quiero, Amalia.
Todavía te quiero.
Siempre te querré."

And I know he is not lying,
only dreaming.
Ay, how I wish I remembered
how to dream this way!
(long pause)

Voice from the dark, like a memory.

MARISA
I'll keep driving if you promise not to stop touching me.

AMALIA *(onstage)*
You want me to stop touching you?

MARISA *(from the dark)*
No.
If you promise *not* to stop.

AMALIA
(long pause)
All I was concerned about
                    was getting my health back together.
It was not so much that I had been sick,
only I lacked energy.
Possibly it was the "change" coming on,
but the women in my familia did not
                    go through the "change"
so young . . . I, not even fifty.

I thought, *maybe it was the American influence*
that causes the blood to be sucked dry from you
so early.
Nothing was wrong with me, really.
My bones ached.   That was it.
I needed rest.

Nothing México couldn't cure, I thought.

(starts to exit)

MARISA
(sitting on the "cliff")
For the whole summer, I watched the people fly
in bright-colored sails over the califas sea
waiting for her.

(AMALIA stops suddenly as if hearing this for the first time, turns, watches MARISA)

MARISA *(to THE PEOPLE)*
Red and gold and blue striped wings with black
letters blazing the sky.
Lifting off the sandy cliffs,
                              dangling gringo legs.

Always imagined myself up there in their place,
flying for real
never coming back
down to earth
leaving
my body
behind.

One morning I awoke to find a bird
dead on the beach.
I knew it wasn't a rock because it was light
enough to roll with the tide.
I saw this from a distance.

Later that day, they found a woman
dead there at the very same spot, I swear.
Una viejita.

A crowd gathered 'round her
as a young man in a blue swimsuit
tried to spoon the sand from her throat
with his finger.
Putting his breath to her was too late.

50

I know it's crazy to say . . .
but I have never seen a dead person.
I mean . . . a live one, just recently dead.
She was so very very grey and wet,
gris y mojada
como la arena.

She was a Mexican
I could tell by her house dress.
How *did* she drown?

(looking to AMALIA)
Then I remembered what Amalia had told me
about omens.
I stopped going
waiting.

AMALIA *(to MARISA)*
(pause) I had a dream once . . .

You and I, Chata, were indias, baking something
maybe bread, maybe clay pots
on a wide expanse of beach.
We were very happy.

And then . . . suddenly . . . the dream changes.
The mood is dark, clouded.
I am in my hut . . . alone.
I remember being crouched down in terror.
In our village, something . . . *(remembering)*
some terrible taboo had been broken.   That was it.
And everyone, in fear for their lives
had returned to their homes.
Suddenly, there is a furious pounding at my door.
"Let me in! Let me in!" And it is *your* voice, Chatita.
But I am unable to move when I realize it is you
who has gone against the code del pueblo.

Funny . . . I was not afraid of being punished.
I was not afraid the gods would enact their wrath
against our pueblo for the breaking of the taboo.
It was merely . . . that the taboo . . . *could* be broken.

And if this law nearly transcribed in blood
could go . . .
then, what else?

What *was* there to hold to?
What immovable truths were left?

Silence.   AMALIA and MARISA look directly at each other, sustain it.

AMALIA   *(to THE PEOPLE)*
Sometimes I think, with me
that she only wanted to feel herself
so much a woman
that she would no longer be hungry for one.
(pause) Pero, siempre tiene hambre.
Siempre tiene pena.

Black out.

Long pause.   As lights gradually come up again, MARISA appears on her "bed," rubbing her calves.
I woke up this morning the same way I have for months.
Sometimes I'm so mad, I can't even hear the birds
                                        outside my window.
I wake instead to this fluttering inside my chest
this heat
like the wings of birds are batting up a war dance
stomping out a fire in there.
(pause) I still wake up imagining touching her . . .
waiting to be touched.

(pause)
I must admit, I wanted to save her.
That's probably the whole truth of the story.
And the problem is . . . sometimes I actually believed
I could and *sometimes* she did, too.
She'd look at me that way, you know, with hope
in her eyes and it would light up her whole face
. . . especially when we made love.
Sometimes that look would make me very nervous
but usually I tried to look past it
tried to get to the heart of the matter
of what we were doing and not get all locked up
thinking about what we were doing.
Thinking always made me nervous and her scared.

When she wasn't thinking, she'd come to me,
I swear, like heat on wheels!
I'd open the door and find her there, wet
from the outta-nowhere June rains
and without her even opening her mouth
I knew what she had come for.

I never knew when to expect her this way
just like the rains
never ever when *I* wanted it asked for it begged for it
only when *she* decided.

But she would lay herself down and wide open for me
like no woman I'd ever had before.
I think it was in the quality of her skin.
Some people, you know, their skin is like a covering.
They're supposed to be showing you something
when the clothes fall into a heap around your four ankles,
but nothing is lost . . . you know what I mean?
They just don' give up nuthin.
Pero Amalia . . . Eeeholay!

She was never fully naked in front of me,
always had to keep some piece of clothing on . . .
a shirt or something always wrapped up around her throat,
her arms all outta it and flying . . .
but she'd never want it all the way off.

What she did reveal, however . . .
each item of clothing removed was a gift,
I swear, a small offering
a *suggestion* of all
that could be lost and found in our making love
together.
It was like she was saying to me,
"I'll lay down my underslip, mi amor . . .
¿y tú? ¿Qué me vas a dar?"
and I'd give her the palm of my hand to warm
the spot she had just exposed.

Everything was a risk.
Everything took time . . . was slow
and painstaking.

55

I'll never forget after the first time we made love
I felt . . . mucho orgullo y todo de eso . . . like a good lover
and she says to me . . .

AMALIA *(from the dark, like a memory)*
You make love to me like worship.

MARISA
and I nearly died, it was so powerful
what she was saying.
And I wanted to say but didn't . . .
"Sí. La mujer es mi religión."
(to herself) If only sex coulda saved us.

You know sometimes when me and her was
                                in the middle of it,
making love . . . I'd look up at her face, kinda grey
from being indoors so much in that cave of a house
                                she lived in.
But when we were together, I'd see it change, turn
this real deep color of brown and olive
like she was cookin inside . . .
(remembering) tan linda.
Kind. Very very very kind to me to herself
                                to the pinche planet
and I'd watch it move from outside the house
where that crazy espíritu of hers had been out makin tracks.

I'd watch it come inside through the door
watch it travel all through her own private miseries
and settle itself finally right there in the room with us.
This bed. *(she pounds it)*
This fucking dreary season.
This cement city.
With us.
With me.
No part of her begging to get outta this.
Have it over.   Forget.

And I could feel all the parts of her move into operation.
Waiting.   Held.   Suspended.
Praying for me to put my mouth to her
and I knew she knew we would find her como fuego
hot hot hot mojada mi mujer
and she could be mi muchachita y mi mujer
en el mismo momento
and just as I pressed my mouth to her, I'd think . . .
I could save your life.

It's not often you get to see people that way
in all their puss and glory
and *still* love them.
It makes you feel so good,
like your hands are weapons of war
and as they move up into el corazón de esta mujer
you are making her body remember

it didn't hafta be that hurt, ¿me entiendes?
It was not natural or right
that she got beat down so damn hard
and that all those crimes had *nothing* to do
with the girl she once was two, three, four
decades ago.

It's like making familia from scratch
each time all over again . . . with strangers
if I must.
If I must, I will.

I am preparing myself for the worst,
so I cling to her in my heart,
my daydream with pencil in my mouth,
when I put my fingers
to my own
forgotten places.

*MARISA slowly rises and exits.   The lights fade out in silence.
Music.*

End of Act Two.

Fin.